Goldilocks and the Three Bears

written by Charlotte Guillain ☆ illustrated by Dawn Beacon

Raintree

Raintree is an imprint of Capstone Global Library Limited, a company incorporated in England and Wales having its registered office at 7 Pilgrim Street, London, EC4V 6LB – Registered company number: 6695582

To contact Raintree please phone 0845 6044371, fax + 44 (0) 1865 312263, or email myorders@raintreepublishers.co.uk. Customers from outside the UK please telephone +44 1865 312262.

First published in 2013

Edited by Daniel Nunn, Rebecca Rissman, and Sian Smith
Designed by Joanna Hinton-Malivoire
Original illustrations © Capstone Global Library Ltd 2013
Illustrated by Dawn Beacon
Production by Victoria Fitzgerald
Originated by Capstone Global Library Ltd
Printed in China

ISBN 978 1 406 25113 5
16 15 14 13 12
10 9 8 7 6 5 4 3 2 1

This book is also available as a big book with the ISBN: 978 1 406 25119 7

British Library Cataloguing in Publication Data
Guillain, Charlotte.
Goldiclucks and the three bears. -- (Animal fairy tales)
1. Children's stories.
I. Title II. Series
823.9'2-dc23

Characters

Goldiclucks

Father Bear

Mother Bear

Baby Bear

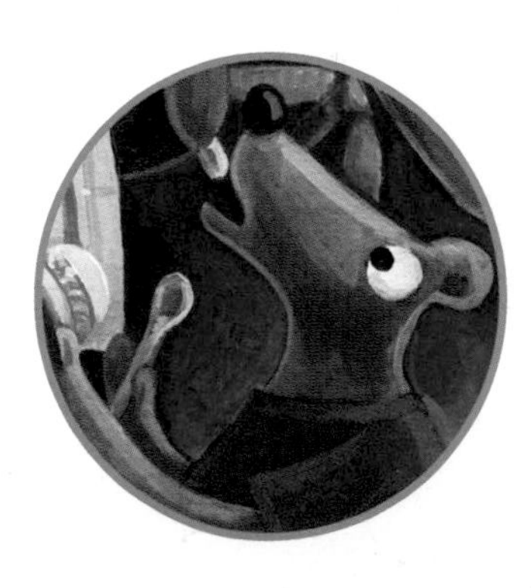

Once upon a time, three bears lived in a beautiful cottage in the woods. One day, Mother Bear made porridge for breakfast. While they waited for their porridge to cool down, the three bears went out to play.

They had not been gone long when a small chick called Goldiclucks arrived and looked in through the window.

Goldiclucks was hungry. When she saw the porridge she went inside to eat some.

The biggest bowl of porridge was too hot.

The middle-sized bowl of porridge was too cold.

But the smallest bowl of porridge was just right, so Goldiclucks gobbled it all up.

Then Goldiclucks saw the three bears' chairs. She tried sitting on the biggest chair but it was too bouncy.

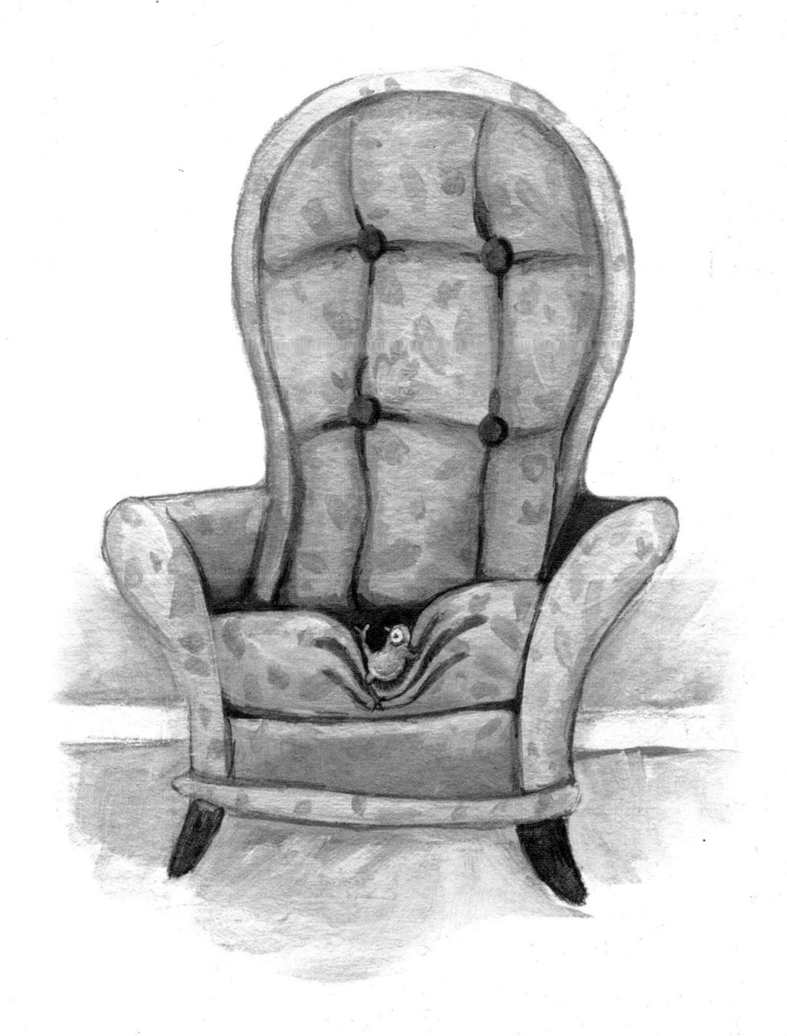

She tried sitting on the middle-sized chair but it was too saggy.

Finally Goldiclucks jumped onto the smallest chair. It was just right.

But just as she landed, there was a loud crack. Goldiclucks had broken it!

CRACK!

Next Goldiclucks saw the three bears' beds. She tried the biggest bed but it was too hard. Then she tried the middle-sized bed, but it was too messy.

Finally, Goldiclucks tried the smallest bed. It was just right. She climbed in and went to sleep.

Soon the three bears came home, ready for their breakfast. But somebody had been eating their porridge!

"My porridge is all gone!" wailed Baby Bear.

Next the bears noticed someone had been sitting on their chairs! "What's this feather doing here?" growled Father Bear.

Suddenly, Baby Bear burst into tears.

"Someone has sat on my chair and broken it!" he cried.

Finally the bears saw their beds.

"Someone has been sleeping in my bed!" shouted Baby Bear.

"And she is **still in it!**"

The three bears roared with anger.

At this, Goldiclucks woke up with a squawk! When she saw the three bears, she flapped out of the window as fast as her little wings could carry her!

And from that day on, the three bears always remembered to lock their doors and windows whenever they went out to play.

The end

Where does this story come from?

You've probably already heard the story that *Goldiclucks and the Three Bears* is based on – *Goldilocks and the Three Bears*. There are many different versions of this story. When people tell a story, they often make little changes to make it their own. How would you change this story?

The history of the story

The *Goldilocks* story was first written down by the poet Robert Southey in 1837, but it had been told by oral storytellers in England for a long time before that. Storytellers entertained people in the days before radio and television.

The original story is called *The Story of the Three Bears* and instead of a little girl, an old woman breaks into the three bears' house. The three bears have gone for a walk and left their porridge to cool. The old woman eats the smallest bear's porridge, breaks his chair, and sleeps in his bed. The bears come back, wake the woman up, and she jumps out of the window and runs away. In other versions of the story, a vixen (a female fox) breaks into the bears' house. It is possible the story then changed to include a little girl called Goldilocks because children liked this more.